P9-DFL-128

Printed in India.

Thumbelina
& The Nightingale
Illustrated by John Patience

Thumbelina

There was once a woman who longed for a child. So desperate was she that she asked for help from a witch who gave her a seed, telling her to watch what happened when she planted it in a flower-pot.

A beautiful flower grew and, when the bud opened, there, inside, was a tiny girl, no bigger than your thumb. The woman loved her dearly and called her Thumbelina.

Thumbelina's bed was a walnut shell and she could row it across a bowl with the aid of horsehairs as oars.

One night when she was asleep in her shell a hideous toad stole her as a bride for his son but a stag beetle rescued her and flew with her to the treetops.

The stag beetle seated Thumbelina on a leaf, brought her a sweet flower to eat and proceeded to pay her compliments. However, when the other beetles came to visit the new arrival they thought her very ugly.

"Oh dear, she has only two legs," said one.

"And no feelers at all," added another.

In truth, Thumbelina was very beautiful but the stag beetle who had taken her began to believe the others and decided to let her go. He flew down to the ground with her, placed her on a daisy and flew away.

Thumbelina was able to find food and shelter in the summer but, when winter came, she was cold and hungry for her clothes were in rags and snow covered her food.

If she had not found the home of a kind field-mouse she would surely have died but the mouse took care of her and, in return, Thumbelina told the mouse and her friend, the old, blind mole, many stories.

The mole fell in love with the tiny girl and dug a tunnel so that she could walk in safety. One day she found a swallow there. It was nearly dead but Thumbelina cared for it till it could fly away.

The mouse was pleased when the mole proposed to Thumbelina and helped her to spin her trousseau but Thumbelina did not want to marry the mole and live underground away from the sun. She went into the sunshine for the last time and asked the flowers to give the swallow her love if ever they saw him again.

Just then there was a joyous "tweet" and there was the swallow. He persuaded Thumbelina to fly on his back to warmer lands.

When they reached the swallow's sunny, summer home the prince of the flower spirits fell in love with Thumbelina and they were married and lived happily ever after.

The Nightingale

Long ago in China there lived an emperor whose palace was the most magnificent in all the world. Close by the palace grew a forest where lived a nightingale who sang so sweetly that even the fishermen would stop their work to listen to its song.

Travellers came from far and wide to see the palace but when they heard the bird singing they declared that it was the loveliest thing of all.

The emperor never left his palace and did not know about the nightingale until he read of it in a book. Then he demanded it be brought to sing

for him. So, that night, the little, brown bird sang in the palace for the great emperor. The nightingale's song was so sweet that tears came to the emperor's eyes and ran down his cheeks.

"That was beautiful," he sobbed. "You must stay in the palace and sing for me whenever I command it."

One day a package arrived for the emperor. It was a gift of a mechanical nightingale from the emperor of Japan made of gold and silver and studded with precious stones. When it was wound up it sang. The song was just as beautiful as the real nightingale's and it could sing it over and over again without becoming tired.

The emperor declared the real nightingale was inferior to the mechanical one and must therefore be banished.

A whole year passed by and then, one night when the mechanical bird was singing, something went 'clang' inside it. It was broken. All kinds of people were called in to mend it but it was completely worn out.

Not long after that the emperor fell ill and it was believed that he would die.

"Oh, little, golden nightingale," he sighed, "sing to me and lighten my heart."

But the mechanical bird remained silent, of course.

All at once a most beautiful song broke the silence. It was the real nightingale who had heard of the emperor's illness. It sat on a branch outside the emperor's window and sang to bring him hope. From that moment the emperor began to recover and soon he was completely well again.